Wings in the Wind

By Julia Walsh

Illustrated by

Karel Hayes and **John Gorey**

Peter E. Randall Publisher
Portsmouth, New Hampshire
2016

In a small town called Newburyport, on the banks of the Merrimack River, lived a little girl named Julie.

Many creatures live along the banks of this river. There is plenty of food, and the tall sea grass makes a perfect place for animals and birds to live and build nests.

Julie loved animals and went to the banks of the river every day to watch the many sea creatures. Her favorite activity, however, was watching and studying the mallard ducks that lived along the river. She had learned about ducks in school and loved to greet the baby ducklings as they hatched from their eggs each spring.

Mallard ducks are beautiful birds. The male ducks, called drakes, are easily recognized by their brilliant green heads and bright yellow beaks, or bills.

The female ducks are called hens. They are mostly brown so they can camouflage, or hide, in order to blend in with the tall grass, grey rocks and mud on the shoreline of the river. The hens are quite lovely, with blue feathers on each wing.

Mallard ducks are migratory birds, which means they fly in flocks to warmer places when the cold New England winter arrives. But they always return with spring, when the mallard hen builds her nest, lays her eggs, and waits for the ducklings to hatch. The mother hen can lay up to 12 eggs, and she sits on them for about three weeks. Once the eggs hatch, the mother hen takes good care of her young—also called her brood.

Julie loved to quietly watch from the docks as the fuzzy little ducklings snuggled with their mother before she led them to the water to teach them to swim. Julie also knew that the mother and her little ducklings must be very careful. Large hungry fish and snapping turtles will sometimes swim up under ducks or ducklings, pull them down into the water, and gobble them up.

One warm evening in early May, Julie took her daily walk, and she spotted something unusual. There were the little ducklings swimming in the river . . . but the mother hen was nowhere to be found.

Now, a mother hen always stays very close to her ducklings to keep them safe and to teach them how to find food. Julie was worried and knew that, without their mother, it would not be easy for these ducklings to survive and grow up.

Every day Julie checked on the little ducklings. Sadly, they were left
to care for themselves, and sadly every day it seemed that one more
of the ducklings had disappeared. Mother ducks will care only for
their own young, and other ducklings are not typically allowed to
join other broods.

Finally there were only two little ducklings left, huddling together one evening. By morning there was only one. The last little duckling crouched in the grass, hiding from any predators that might want to eat him. Julie knew he must be feeling very lonely and scared.

Now, there had been many ducklings that hatched that spring and followed their mothers closely. Even though this last duckling was all alone, he still did all his duckling duties. Every day he searched alone for food, and every night he hid alone in the grass to sleep. When he would try to approach other duck families, they squawked and sent him away.

He was very brave, and he was doing his very best, but he still had a lot to learn about growing up to become a drake. Besides, Julie knew that ducks do not live alone—they live in groups. After growing up with their brothers and sisters, ducks join a flock to safely migrate south for the winter.

Even though the last duckling was not welcomed into a brood, he would not give up. Every day he followed the other broods as they went to feed. He dug into the muddy banks of the Merrimack to eat worms, and he dug up the roots of the sea grass and gobbled them up, too. He even learned to dive under water to catch small fish . . . a tasty treat for a duck that is willing to be brave and try something new!

As spring turned to summer, the last duck grew strong and healthy. The hot sun warmed the river and the long days gave plenty of time for the ducklings to grow into young drakes and hens. In fact, Julie noticed that her friend was showing hints of emerald green on his head. He had become a young drake. But Julie knew he would need to join a flock, and she still worried about him.

Every day and every night the brave young drake stayed close to the other families. Some were forming groups in the water. He would swim close, circling around them, and he would sleep close by. But when he got too close, they would quickly send him off, flapping their wings while snapping their beaks and honking as they chased him away.

One Sunday, Julie was not able to take her usual walk to the river. Her family was going to visit Nana and Papa. Julie loved these visits. She loved their warm house full of old pictures and Nana's homemade cookies.

At her grandparents' house, Julie loved to look at the pictures of her own mother when she was a girl, and the pictures of her aunts and uncles and cousins. She loved to see Nana when she was a teenager wearing her party dresses.

On this Sunday, Julie saw something she had not noticed before. She saw a picture of Papa in front of a fighter plane, wearing a soldier's uniform. Julie knew Papa had been in the war where he had seen many sad things he did not talk about. Even though he was smiling in the picture, Julie recognized the lonely look in Papa's eyes in the photograph. That look reminded her of the young drake.

Papa walked over and put his arm around Julie. They stood together quietly looking at the old photograph. Julie told him about the young drake and how she was very worried about him because he did not have a flock.

Papa looked into Julie's eye. He said, very kindly and thoughtfully, "We all need to find our flock in life, but don't give up on the drake yet. Friendship can sometimes come in the most wonderful ways."

"Besides," he told her, "the river is a special place. Tides come in and out, the seasons come and go. Nature moves in a kind of rhythm, but no matter what, goodness, love, is like the wind. It is always there for us, even if we can't see it." Then, giving Julie a wink, he said, "And you never know what it will bring."

On the way home Julie thought about what Papa had said. She wondered, *what did Papa mean? What would the wind bring? Would the drake find his flock?*

The summer nights began to feel chilly. The male ducklings grew into brightly colored drakes with green heads, white collars, and bright yellow bills. The female ducklings, now young hens, kept their brown color and had beautiful blue bands of wing feathers. The young drake was now a brave mallard.

All the mallard ducks had grown strong and healthy, having enjoyed the rich feeding grounds of the Merrimack River all summer. They were preparing for their journey to their winter home further south. The ducks recognized the change in the sun's angle and light and knew winter was coming. They were born with this skill, called an instinct.

As fall approached, Julie realized that the brave mallard would soon need to move to a warm home for the winter so he could find food. She had read that mallards, even with their powerful beaks, cannot break through the winter ice to get food, and they certainly cannot swim underwater to get food beneath the patches of ice.

As she saw the drake preparing for the journey south, she was hoping with all her heart he would have a flock to join to make the long trip. Julie thought that flocks liked to leave at sunrise, and she wanted to be able to say goodbye; so she listened every morning just before sunrise, trying to hear the sounds of mallards preparing to make their journey south. One morning she heard the restless fluttering of wings and squawks as the flock of mallards called to each other, gathering and getting ready to slip away. Julie raced to the window to watch.

By the time she got to the window, the flock was gone. But sadly, there, alone in the tall golden grass, stood the young brave mallard. The flock had left him behind.

He swam quietly that day, all alone on the river. Julie cried and wanted to be alone, too. Even the river was silent and seemed to weep. All was still.

As time went on, the winds picked up, leaves fluttered and danced, and the golden sea grass waved. The beauty of fall was everywhere. Then one day, while children hurried to school, a most exciting thing happened. A different flock of mallards arrived from further north. They needed to eat and to rest along their journey south.

When Julie got home from school she took her daily walk to the riverbank and found it alive with excitement! She was thrilled to see the new flock of mallards busy feeding and swimming in and out of the docks. Julie quickly looked for the drake, and what she saw filled her with joy. Papa was right! Friendship can come in the most wonderful ways.

When the new ducks met the drake, they fluttered and circled around him like he was one of their own. They seemed very impressed by his particularly bright green collar, his proud air, and his brave deeds as he navigated the river. He graciously showed his new friends the best spots to eat and the safest places to sleep.

At the library, Julie learned that northern mallards will continue flying south, as New England shores usually become bitter cold. But the northern flock never left the Merrimack River to fly south. The winter was unusually mild, so bitter freezes were rare and the ducks were able to find plenty of food.

So the ducks wintered in Newburyport. One day when Julie took her walk, she noticed the drake had found a hen— so now he had his own mate. Julie's heart was full of joy as she now had two friends on the river.

Early, dark winter evenings changed into late, glowing dusks. The air became warmer and the days longer. Julie watched the season change and waited for the flock to return north. Early in March, mallards return to their nesting grounds. A female duck always returns to the same spot to build her nest and raise her young. She knew the proud mallard would be joining his new mate. While the flock prepared for their journey, Julie prepared herself to say goodbye.

Early one dawn when the wind shifted, Julie was drawn to the window. As if responding to one lovely call, the flock ascended in flight. This time the drake was part of the group. Her dear friend had found his flock and was going home, wings in the wind.

Author JULIA WALSH grew up in Delaware. She loved to study wildlife as she explored the Chesapeake Bay area with her grandfather and his prized Labradors. The author holds degrees in occupational therapy from Boston University and counseling and school psychology from Immaculata University. She has worked in private and public schools as a therapist and educator. The author currently resides in Newburyport where she loves to observe the beauty of nature along the banks of the Merrimack River. Visit her website: www.JuliaWalshAuthor.com

Award winning and *New York Times* reviewed author and illustrator KAREL HAYES has written and illustrated six books and illustrated over twenty-five books, four of them with her son and fellow artist, JOHN GOREY. Her artwork has been shown in several art clubs in New York City, The Cincinnati Museum of Natural History, the Philadelphia Museum of Fine Arts Sales Gallery and in many other galleries throughout the U.S.

ISBN13: 978-1-942155-11-9

Library of Congress Control Number: 2016930076

Published by
Peter E. Randall Publisher
Portsmouth, New Hampshire 03801
www.perpublisher.com

Book Design: Grace Peirce